FRANKENSTEIN

MARY SHELLEY

ADAPTED BY

Emily Hutchinson

SADDLEBACK PUBLISHING, INC.

The Adventures of Huckleberry Finn
The Call of the Wild
A Christmas Carol
Frankenstein
The Red Badge of Courage
The Scarlet Letter
A Tale of Two Cities
Treasure Island

Development and Production: Laurel Associates, Inc.
Cover and Interior Art: Black Eagle Productions

SADDLEBACK PUBLISHING, INC.
3505 Cadillac Ave., Building F-9
Costa Mesa, CA 92626-1443

ISBN 1-56254-264-8

Printed in the United States of America
05 04   9 8 7 6 5 4 3 2 1

CONTENTS

Opening Letter

To: Mrs. Saville, England
August 5, 17__

Dear Sister,

First, I want to tell you that I am alive and well. My dream of traveling to the North Pole seems closer than ever to being fulfilled. But second, I want to tell you a strange story about what has been happening.

Our ship is nearly closed in by ice and fog. Now and then the seas churn, and huge chunks of ice break up. The other day, I stood looking out over the vast plains of ice. Suddenly, about half a mile away, I saw a dog sled going north. The figure in the carriage had the shape of a man, but it was the size of a giant. He was gone before I could see more.

The next morning, we came upon a second sled. Only one dog remained alive. There was a man, nearly frozen, in the sled. We got him on board and carried him to my cabin. I never saw a man in so wretched a condition. Two days passed before he was able to speak. We have become friends. He is a kind, intelligent, gentle, and well-educated man. I am very fond of him. Something, however, is troubling him deeply.

Last night, he told me that he has a story to tell me. Tomorrow, he will begin it. I plan to write it down in his own words as much as possible.

Your loving brother,

R. Walton

1 Frankenstein Begins His Story

My name is Victor Frankenstein. I grew up in Geneva, Switzerland. My family is one of the best-known families there. For a long time I was my parents' only child. But that changed when I was about five years old.

My parents passed a week at Lake Como in Italy. My mother was always interested in helping the poor. One day, they visited a poor farmer who had five hungry children.

One of the children, a little girl named Elizabeth, attracted my mother more than the others. She wasn't like the other children in looks or in personality. The farmer's wife told my mother about the girl. She was not their child, but the daughter of a nobleman. The girl's mother had died, and her father had put her in the farmer's care. The father then went off to war and had not been heard from since. Since then, hard times had come to the farmer. He had very little money and four children of his own.

My mother had always wanted a little girl. She asked the farmer if she and my father could adopt the girl. Although the farmer and his wife loved the child, they knew she would have a much happier life with my family. So they let my parents take Elizabeth.

Soon Elizabeth Lavenza became more than my sister. She became the beautiful and adored companion of my childhood. We called each other "cousin" and shared a deep love until the day she died.

When I was seven years old, my brother Ernest was born. At that time my parents gave up their travels and stayed home. We had a house in Geneva. We also had a place in the country, on the shore of a lake, where we stayed most of the time. It was here that my brother William was born.

Our family did not know a lot of people. I had one close friend, Henry Clerval, the son of a Geneva merchant. Henry, Elizabeth, and I were like three parts of one person. Elizabeth was the soul, Henry was the heart, and I was the mind. Henry told stories of heroes and great adventurers. Elizabeth had her art. And I began to study science.

When I was 13, my father found me reading one of the books in his library. "Ah, you're reading *this*?" he said. "My dear Victor, do not waste your time. This is sad trash." If only my father had explained that no one believed in these books anymore, everything might have been different. Science had already proved that these ideas were silly, but I didn't know this. I was angry. My father thought the books I liked were trash! Instead of taking his advice, I found more books like them.

Looking back on it, I know that I was foolish. I tried using spells to change lead into gold. I tried to raise ghosts. Of course, none of these spells worked. I might have gone on this way for years, but then an accident happened that changed my life.

When I was about 15 years old, we were at our country house. A violent and terrible storm came up. As I stood at the door, I saw lightning hit an old and beautiful oak. As soon as the light vanished, the oak had disappeared. Nothing remained but a blasted stump. The next morning, I saw that the tree was reduced to thin ribbons of wood. I never saw anything so completely destroyed.

A friend of my father's was visiting us that day. He was a scientist. He explained a theory of his on the subject of electricity. This was new and astonishing to me. What he said made my earlier studies seem foolish. It seemed to me as if nothing would or could ever be known. So I gave up the study of science and immediately began to study mathematics.

When I look back, it seems to me that this change of attitude was caused by a guardian angel. It was perhaps the last effort of that angel to save my life.

It was a strong effort of the spirit of good, but it did no good. Destiny was too strong. Her laws had already sealed my terrible fate.

§ 2 Frankenstein Learns the Secret of Life

When I was 17, my parents said that I should begin my studies at a university in Germany. But before I could leave, the first sorrow of my life came. It was an omen of my future misery.

My mother became ill with scarlet fever. On her deathbed, she called Elizabeth and me to her side. "My children," she said, "I have always wanted you to be married one day. This hope will now be a comfort to your father. I regret that I am being taken from you. I pray that we will meet in another world."

She died calmly. We were all grief-stricken. I stayed home for a few more weeks. Finally, it was time for me to leave. My friend Henry spent the last evening with Elizabeth and me. The three of us had never felt closer. None of us knew that we would never be as happy again. I left the next day.

After a long, hard trip, I arrived in Germany. The next day I went to the university and met one of my professors, Dr. Krempe. He was a rude man, but he knew a lot about science. He asked me what science books I had read. I mentioned the books about magic spells. "Have you really spent your time studying such nonsense?" he said. "You'll have to start your studies all over again."

About a week later, I stopped by the lecture hall to meet Dr. Waldman, the chemistry professor. He was about 50, a kindly man. He was everything Krempe was not. His voice was the sweetest I had ever heard. And he was a good teacher. He started off with a history of chemistry:

"The old masters promised things they could not do: turn lead into gold, stay young forever. These were all empty dreams. Scientists today are different. They don't promise much, but look at what they have done! We know how the blood moves through our bodies. We know what makes up the air we breathe. Who knows what wonders may come next?"

The professor's words filled my mind with one thought. So much has been done, but I shall achieve even more. I will show the world the deepest mysteries of creation.

From that day, chemistry became the most important thing in my life. I read books, attended lectures, and got to know the science professors. I often studied so hard that the stars disappeared in the light of morning while I was still in my lab.

Two years passed in this manner. I paid no visit to Geneva, for I was too busy with my studies. None but those who have experienced it can understand how exciting science can be. There is constant food for discovery and wonder.

I decided to study human biology. To study life is also to study death. I wanted to see how death changes the human body. I cut into dead animals and people. I saw how death gives way to life. A human or animal dies, and its body gives food and life to worms. Then, like a flash of light, the answer to the secret of life came to me.

I am not a madman. As sure as the sun shines, all that I am telling you is true. *I became able to make lifeless matter come to life!*

Ah! I can see by the look on your face, my friend, that you expect me to tell you the secret. That cannot be. Listen to my story, and you will know why I will remain silent on that subject. Learn from my example how dangerous knowledge can be.

When I found I really could create life, I had to stop and think. How could I prepare a frame for it? I knew it would be too hard to work on very small parts. So I decided to make a being of gigantic size—that is, about eight feet tall. After collecting my materials, I was ready to begin.

Who can imagine the horrors of my secret work? I found my supplies in graveyards, dissecting rooms, and slaughterhouses. I can still see all those staring, dead eyes. I often turned with loathing from my work. But, eager to succeed, I kept on.

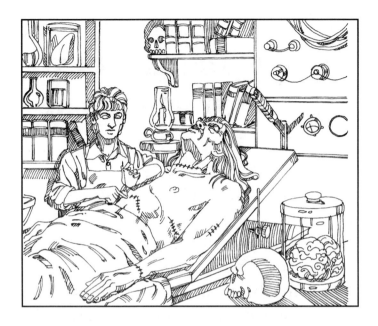

My work became everything to me. I didn't write to my family, and I never went out with friends. A year went by. I missed all the changes of the seasons. I was working so hard that I began to feel ill. My purpose alone kept me going. I knew that my labors would soon end. I promised myself exercise and amusement as soon as my creation was complete.

§3 The Creature Comes to Life

It was on a dreary night in November that my work came to an end. I arranged my instruments around me, so I could bring to life the lifeless thing that lay at my feet. It was already one in the morning. The rain pattered against the window. My candle was nearly burned out. Then, by the low light, I saw the dull yellow eyes of the creature open. It breathed hard. Its arms and legs shook.

How can I describe this creature I had worked so hard to make? He was very tall. I had chosen his face as beautiful. *Beautiful!* How wrong could I have been? His skin barely covered the muscles beneath. His hair was shiny, black, and flowing. His teeth were white and perfect. But these things only made the rest of him seem more horrid. His watery eyes were almost the same color as their white sockets. His skin was dry, and his lips were straight and black.

I had worked hard for nearly two years. For this I had lost rest and health. Now that I had finished, the dream vanished. Horror and disgust filled my heart. I rushed out of the lab and ran to my bedroom. I could not sleep, so I paced the floor.

Still dressed, I threw myself on the bed. My sleep was disturbed by wild dreams about Elizabeth. She was young, healthy, and beautiful. But when I took her in my arms to kiss her—she changed. Her face looked dead. I thought I held the body of my dead mother in my arms. I could see worms crawling in the folds of her dress.

I woke up with a start. The dim, yellow light of the moon came through my bedroom window. Then I saw the creature—the miserable monster I had created. He held up the curtain of the bed. His eyes were fixed on me. From his mouth came an awful sound, while a grin formed on his face. He might have spoken, but I did not hear. One hand reached out, but I escaped and rushed

downstairs. For the rest of the night I walked back and forth in the yard.

When morning came, I began roaming through town. I had no idea where I was or what I was doing. I did not dare return to my apartment. Finally, I came to an inn where stagecoaches stopped. One was coming in from Geneva. As I watched, the door opened and I saw Henry Clerval. Upon seeing me, my friend exclaimed, "My dear Frankenstein! How glad I am to see you! How lucky that you should be here to meet me!"

Suddenly, for the first time in months, I felt calm joy. It was almost as good as being back home. I welcomed my friend warmly, and we started walking toward my apartment. Clerval told me that his father had finally agreed to let him go to college.

"I am so glad to see you," I said. "But tell me, how is my family?"

"Very well, and very happy. They just wonder why you never write. But, my dear Frankenstein," he said, as he stopped and looked into my face. "I did not notice before how ill you look. You are so thin and pale. You look as if you haven't been sleeping."

"You have guessed right. I have been too busy to sleep. But I hope that my work is now at an end and that I am finally free."

I didn't dare say more about my work. I didn't want anyone to know about it. We arrived at my apartment building. I then realized that the creature might still be upstairs, alive and walking about. I dreaded to see the monster, but I feared still more that Henry should see him. I asked Henry to wait a few minutes at the bottom of the stairs. I ran up, threw the door open, and checked inside. Nothing was there. I could hardly believe it. When I was sure that the apartment was empty, I clapped my hands for joy and ran down to Clerval.

We went up to my room, and the servant brought us breakfast. As we ate, my pulse began to beat fast. I could not stay still. I jumped over the chairs, clapped my hands, and laughed aloud. When Clerval saw the wild look in my eyes, he was astonished.

"Victor," he said. "What's the matter?"

"Do not ask me," I cried. I threw my hands in front of my eyes, for I thought I saw the creature come into the room. "*He* can tell you. Oh, save me! Save me!" I fell to the floor in a fit. It was the beginning of a nervous fever that lasted for months.

Henry took care of me during the time. I later learned that he did not tell my family about it, to spare them the grief. Little by little, I started to get better. I began to see things around me and to talk with Henry.

When I was finally well, Henry told me that classes were about to begin at the university. I knew that I didn't want to study science again. Every time I thought about science, I remembered where it had led me. So, for the next six months, I went to Henry's classes with him. We studied literature, languages, and history.

Finally the school year ended. I looked forward to returning to Geneva. But bad weather damaged the roads and prevented me from leaving right away. It was another six months before I could go home. Before I left, Henry suggested a walking tour. Wanting to bid a personal farewell to Germany, I was happy to agree. I was fond of exercise, and Clerval had always been my favorite walking companion.

We passed two weeks walking through the countryside. It restored my health and spirits. I became the same happy man who, a few years ago, had no sorrow or care. The beauty of nature again filled me with joy.

We returned to the college on a Sunday afternoon. The peasants were dancing, and everyone we met seemed happy. I, too, was full of happiness that day.

§ 4 The Creature's First Victims

On my return, I found the following letter from my father:

My dear Victor,

I hardly know how to tell you this, son. William is dead! That sweet child, who was so gentle! Victor, he is murdered!

We had all been walking near Lake Geneva when we discovered that William was lost. He had been playing hide-and-seek with Ernest, but Ernest could not find him.

About five in the morning I found my lovely boy. The print of the murderer's finger was on his neck. He had been wearing a pin with a portrait of your mother on it. The pin is gone! Doubtless it was the temptation that made the murderer commit this deed.

Come home, dearest Victor. You alone can console Elizabeth.

Your loving and grieving father,
Alphonse Frankenstein

Within hours, I had said farewell to Clerval and was on my way to Geneva. My journey was very sad. As I drew closer to home, grief and fear overcame me. It was completely dark when I arrived in Geneva. The gates of the city were already shut. I had to pass the night at a village outside the city. I was unable to rest, so I decided to visit the spot where my poor William had been murdered. I could not go through the town, so I crossed the lake in a boat.

As I rowed, I saw lightning flash on a nearby mountain. The storm came in fast. On landing, I climbed a low hill so I could watch its progress. While I watched the storm, I walked on. I clasped my hands and cried out loud, "William, dear angel!" As I said these words, a flash of lightning showed me a figure in the woods. Its huge size instantly told me that it was the wretch to whom I had given life.

What was he doing here? Could he be the murderer of my brother? No sooner did that idea cross my mind than I knew it was true. The figure passed me quickly, and I lost it in the gloom. I tried to follow, but he was too fast. A minute later, lightning flashed again. I saw the creature climbing. The cliff was almost straight up and down, but he rose up the steep slope with ease.

Two years had passed since he first received life. Was this his first crime? I had no way of knowing. I spent that night, cold and wet, in the open air. I thought about the being I had let loose upon mankind. What horrors would he commit?

Day dawned, and I hurried to my father's house. My first thought was to tell what I knew of the murderer. But then I thought about the awful story I had to tell. A being whom I myself had created had met me at midnight on a steep mountain! I knew that if anyone else said such a thing to me, I would have thought it the ravings of a madman. Besides, he would be impossible to catch. Who could arrest such a strong, gigantic creature? I decided to remain silent.

Six years had passed since I last saw my family. Ernest met me at the door.

"Welcome, my dearest Victor!" he said. "Your presence will, I hope, console our father and poor Elizabeth. Poor William! He was our darling and our pride!"

Tears fell from my brother's eyes. "Elizabeth needs you most of all. She feels responsible for the death of William. But since the murderer has been discovered—"

"The murderer *discovered*? How can that be? Who could catch him? One might as well try to catch the winds."

"I do not know what you mean," said Ernest. "To us, the discovery we have made completes our misery. Who could believe that Justine Moritz could have done it? She was always so fond of all the family. All these years that she has lived with us, she was more than a servant. She was a friend."

"Justine Moritz! Poor, poor girl. Is she the accused? But it must be wrong.

Everyone must know that. Who could believe it, Ernest?"

"No one did at first. But the evidence is strong. The trial is today."

He told me that Justine became ill on the morning William's body had been found. She had been in bed for several days. During this time, one of the servants was tending the clothes she had worn that night. The pin William had been wearing was in Justine's pocket. On being accused, the poor girl couldn't explain how she got it.

This was a strange tale, but it did not shake my faith. I said, "You are all wrong. I *know* the murderer. Justine is innocent."

Just then, my father entered. I saw his unhappiness, but still he tried to welcome me cheerfully. We were soon joined by Elizabeth. She welcomed me with great affection. "Your arrival, dear cousin, fills me with hope. Maybe you can find some way to prove Justine's innocence."

"She *is* innocent, my Elizabeth. That will be proved. Fear nothing," I said.

"Dearest niece," said my father, "dry your tears. If Justine is innocent, I am sure the truth will come out."

But the trial did not prove Justine's innocence. She told the court that she had spent that evening at an aunt's house, about three miles from Geneva. While she was walking back home at about 9:00, she met a man. He asked her if she had seen the child who was lost. When she found out the child was William, she spent several hours searching for him. But by then, the gates of Geneva had been shut. So she spent the rest of the night in a barn. She barely slept. Then, a few minutes before morning, some heavy footsteps disturbed her, and she awoke. She went back to the Frankenstein home, where she lived. As for the pin, she had no explanation for it.

Elizabeth even took the stand to tell the court about Justine's fine character. But that did not help. Justine was found guilty. Two days later she was hanged.

I saw the deep grief of my Elizabeth. This sadness was also my doing! My father's woe, the sorrow of my home—all was the work of my hands! I was torn by remorse, horror, and despair. My family's sorrow was all my fault. Later that day, I wept upon the graves of William and Justine. They were the first victims of my unholy arts.

# Frankenstein Meets the Creature

No words can describe how I felt after the deaths of William and Justine. I thought back on my life and felt nothing but guilt and remorse. I had started out with good intentions. I only wanted to be useful to my fellow beings. Now all was ruined!

This state of mind changed me. I avoided all company. The sounds of joy were torture to me. I started spending more and more time alone.

My father saw how I had changed. He tried to help me. "Do you think, Victor," he said, "that I do not suffer also? No one could love a child more than I loved your brother." Tears came to his eyes. I could answer my father with only a look of despair.

About this time we moved to our other house at Belrive. I was glad about this. The shutting of the Geneva gates at 10:00 P.M. had kept me from staying on the lake after that hour. I was now free. Often, after the rest of the family had gone to bed, I took the boat out on the water. Sometimes I was tempted to plunge into the silent lake and drown. But I thought about how my family was suffering. Should I desert them, and leave them exposed to the fiend I had created?

At these moments I wept bitterly and wished for peace. But that could not be. *I* was the cause of terrible evils. I lived in daily fear that the monster might commit some new crime. And I had a feeling that all was not over. There was always reason for fear so long as anyone I loved remained behind. My hatred of this fiend cannot possibly be imagined. I would have climbed to the highest mountain peak, if I could have thrown him to the base.

Our house was the house of mourning. My father was ill from sorrow, and Elizabeth was not herself. She no longer enjoyed the beauty of nature. "My dear Victor," she said, "when I think about Justine, I no longer see the world as a good place. William and Justine were murdered, and the murderer escapes. He walks about the world free. But even if I were condemned to hang for the same crimes, I would not change places with such a wretch."

I listened to Elizabeth with great agony. Not in deed, but in effect, *I* was the true murderer. I drew near to her, as if in terror. I was afraid that at any minute the destroyer would rob me of her.

Nothing could save me from my despair. Even love had no effect. I was surrounded by a dark cloud. Sometimes I felt driven to seek exercise and a change of place. One day, I suddenly left my home and headed toward the Alpine valley of Chamounix.

It was August, nearly two months after the death of Justine. As I listened to the sound of the river raging among the rocks, I began to feel better. The dashing of the waterfalls, the ruined castles, the charming little cottages here and there among the trees—all were beautiful to me. Most beautiful of all were the mighty Alps.

A tingling, long-lost sense of pleasure sparked within me during this journey. At last I arrived at the village of Chamounix. I got a room and stood at the window. Watching the lightning in the mountains, I again listened to the rushing river. This sound acted as a lullaby. When I placed my head upon my pillow, I slept soundly.

I spent the following morning roaming through the valley and climbing a nearby mountain. It was raining, but I didn't care. I wanted a long, hard walk. It was nearly noon when I got to the top. I looked down on all the beauty below me. I felt good.

Suddenly I saw the figure of a man in the distance. He was running toward me with superhuman speed. As he came closer, I saw that it was the wretch I had created! I trembled with rage and horror.

"Devil!" I exclaimed. "Aren't you afraid that I will kill you? If only your death would bring back to life the innocent victims you have murdered!"

The monster did not try to harm me. He only said, "I thought you'd act like this.

People always hate the wretched. And I am the most wretched of all living things! Even the lowest man on earth is loved by his creator. Yet you—*my* creator—hate me! I want only one thing. If you will do what I ask, I promise to leave you at peace. But if you refuse my request, I will kill all of your remaining friends."

"Hated monster! Come closer, so that I may end your wretched life." I jumped at him, but he easily got away from me.

"Will nothing move you to help me? Hear me out, Frankenstein. Even the guilty, by human laws, are allowed to speak in their own defense. I have no one who loves me. Everyone's hand is raised against me. And it is not my fault. You must hear my tale."

I thought about what the creature was saying. I was his creator. Maybe I did owe him some happiness. Perhaps I should listen to what he had to say. The creature told me to follow him. He led me to a hut a few hundred feet below the mountaintop. There, he told me his story.

The Creature Tells of His Early Life

6

"It is hard for me to remember the early days of my life. I saw, felt, heard, and smelled at the same time. I could hardly tell one sensation from another. I know now what I was experiencing. I was born fully grown—but I was like a newborn baby!

"When you ran from me, I didn't know why. How could I know how ugly I was? Without knowing why, I took a coat from your house, and I left. I went deep into the woods. I slept on the wet ground. I ate what I could find—mostly berries at first.

"I was cold, hungry, and thirsty. Several days passed, and all I knew was light, hunger, thirst, and darkness. All this time I was sad, but I didn't know why.

"My sensations began to be more distinct. Every day my mind received new

34

ideas. My eyes became used to the light. I could tell the difference between insects and plants, and, later, one plant from another.

"One day I found what was left of a campfire. I was delighted with the warmth I felt. In my joy, I touched it, but quickly found out that it could burn me. I looked at the material of the fire and found that it was wood. I collected some branches and soon learned how to make a fire and keep it going.

"Food was hard to find. Often, after spending a whole day searching, I would find only acorns to eat. I decided to go somewhere else, where there might be more food. I started walking through the woods to the open country. A great fall of snow had taken place the night before. The fields were all white. I found my feet chilled by the snow.

"I traveled across the fields for hours. At sunset, I arrived at a small village. How miraculous did this appear! There were vegetables in gardens and milk and cheese placed in some windows. I tried to enter a cottage, but when the villagers saw me, they attacked me. Finally, bruised by stones,

I ran back to the open countryside.

"That night I hid in a shed, which was joined to a neat cottage. But after my last experience, I dared not enter it. The shed was dry. I found it a good shelter from the snow, rain, and the cruelty of man.

"In the morning, I found a small crack in the cottage wall. That night, hiding in the shed again, I looked through the crack at the people inside. There I saw an old man, a young man, and a young woman.

"These people had a way to make a room bright at night! The candles were wonderful. And the old man did something that was even more wonderful. He played a guitar and sang. At first, I didn't know what the instrument was. But, oh, the music! It was beautiful!

"The young man and woman sang along. I'd never heard the sweet sound of singing before. These three people seemed to have everything. It was sad to think of what I had—bare ground to sleep on and no one to love or care for me.

"Later I learned that the family was very poor. The two young people often gave their food to the old man because there wasn't enough for all of them.

"I spent most of the winter in the shed. I didn't know what language was until I heard these people make sounds to each other. I wanted to learn how to talk.

"Slowly, I began to learn words. My first words were *fire, milk, bread,* and *wood.* As I learned to speak and understand, I found out more about the people in the cottage. They all had names. The girl was called *sister* or *Agatha*. The boy was called *brother* or *Felix*. They called the old man *Father*.

"The more I watched these people, the more I cared about them. When they were unhappy, I felt sad. When they were happy, I also felt happy. I admired their beautiful faces. Their bodies were graceful and delicate. But how terrified I was when I saw myself in a pool of water! At first I did not believe it was I who was reflected there. When I realized it was, I was filled with sorrow and shame.

"I tried to help the people by clearing snow from their path and collecting wood. Then I began to think about showing myself to them. I knew I would have to learn how to speak first. In the forest, I began to practice the few words I understood. As spring approached, I was beginning to hope for a happy future."

7 The Creature Continues His Tale

"The weather in the spring became fine and the skies cloudless. My senses were refreshed by a thousand sights of beauty. Then, on one of these lovely spring days, someone tapped at the door of the cottage.

"It was a lady on horseback, escorted by a guide. The lady was dressed in a dark suit. Her head was covered with a thick black veil. Felix seemed very happy to see her. Every sign of sorrow left his face, and his eyes sparkled. When she held out her hand to him, he bent to kiss it and called her *sweetheart*.

"Her name was Safie. Somehow, Felix was different with her than he was with Agatha. It took me some time to figure out why. It was the first time I had seen a man and woman in love.

"I soon saw that the stranger did not speak the same words the family did. I could see that she was trying to learn their language. The idea came to me that I, too, should make use of the instructions. When Safie got her lessons in French, I watched and listened. That is how I learned to speak, read, and write.

"From listening to Safie talk with Felix and Agatha, I learned a lot about the family. Their last name was De Lacey. They were from France. At one time, they had been rich. Safie's father was a good friend of the family. But Safie's father had gotten into bad trouble with the government. The De Laceys tried to help him, but that got them into trouble, too. They lost everything they had. They had to run away to Germany and live in this small cottage.

"Safie and Felix were very much in love. They had been planning to marry. So it was hard on Felix when they were separated. That is why Felix had always seemed so unhappy. Then, Safie's father died, and Safie had come to live with the De Laceys.

"The lessons that Felix gave to Safie were very interesting to me. While I improved in language, I also learned about history—for Felix based his lessons on a history book. I learned about the systems of human society, such as division of property. I learned that some people have great wealth and others live in deepest poverty. I learned that the most valued qualities are good family background and money. A man might be respected with only *one* of these things. But without *both*, he was doomed to waste his powers for the profits of the chosen few.

"And what was I? I had no money, no friends, no family, no property. Besides that, I was hideous and ugly. I was not even of the same nature as man. I was stronger and less affected by the extremes of heat and cold. When I looked around, I saw none like me. Was I, then, truly a monster—from which all men would run?

"I cannot tell you the agony that these thoughts brought to me. I tried to put the ideas out of my head, but I could not. Other ideas were impressed upon me even more deeply. I heard about the difference between men and women, and the birth and growth of children. I learned how family members loved one another. I learned about all the relationships that bind people together.

"But where were *my* friends and relations? No father had watched over my infant days. No mother had blessed me with smiles and caresses. As long as I could remember, I had been the same height and size. I had never yet seen a being that looked like me. What *was* I? The question came to me again and again, to be answered only with groans."

8 The Creature's Request

"Not long after I learned to read, I found a box in the woods. There were three books in it. Luckily, the books were written in French—the language I had learned.

"Until that time, all I knew of the world was what I had seen in the cottage. Now I learned what life was like outside the De Lacey family. I learned about human feelings. I also learned some history.

"One book told about an all-powerful God at war with His heavenly creatures. Then I read about the creation of Adam. I wondered about my own creator. Had he turned from me, as God had from Satan?

"Then I read another book. It was in the pocket of the coat I had taken from your lab, Frankenstein. Now that I could read, I opened it. It was your journal of the four months before my creation.

"I now know what an evil person you are. Why did you form a monster so hideous that even *you* turned away in disgust? How I hate the day that I received life! Even Satan had companions. But I am alone and hated.

"But wait—there is more to my story. One beautiful autumn day, Agatha, Felix, and Safie went for a walk. The old man was alone. I had learned why the young people helped him so much—he was blind. I knew that he could not see how ugly I was. Perhaps I could talk to him. I don't know how long I stood at the cottage door, afraid to knock. I almost ran away a few times. Finally, I tapped on the door.

" 'Come in,' said the old man.

"I stepped inside. 'Pardon me,' I said to De Lacey. 'I am a tired traveler in need of rest. May I sit a few minutes by your fire?'

" 'Of course,' the old man said.

"I sat down. The old man said, 'You speak my language. Are you French?'

" 'No,' I said. 'But I was taught by a French family. I have come here to see them.

They are wonderful people, but they have never seen me. I am afraid they will reject me. Then I will have no friends at all.'

" 'Do not despair. If these people are as good as you say, they will welcome you.'

"I told De Lacey that I was not very pleasant to look at. I was afraid the family would only see how ugly I was on the outside. They might not be able to see me as a loving and kind friend.

" 'Where do these friends live?'

" 'Near this spot,' I said.

"The old man said, 'I cannot judge your looks, but you sound sincere. Perhaps I can be of use. Who are these friends?'

"Just as I was about to answer, the young people returned. My heart was filled with fear. I cried, 'Save and protect me! You and your family are the friends whom I seek!'

" 'Great God!' exclaimed the old man. 'Who are you?' Just then, the cottage door opened, and the young people came in. Agatha fainted, and Safie ran screaming from the cottage. Felix tore me away from the old man, to whose knees I clung. He

picked up a stick and began to hit me. I could have torn him to pieces, but I did not. With tears in my eyes, I ran from the cottage.

"I spent the night hiding in the woods. Once the sun came up, I began to think more clearly. I was a fool to have let the young people see me. I should have made several short visits to old De Lacey, so he could have prepared his family to meet me. Perhaps it was not too late to undo the damage.

"That night, I went back to the cottage and hid in the shed. I waited for the hour when the family arose. That hour passed, and the family did not appear. Later that morning, I saw Felix approach the cottage with another man. The stranger seemed angry. 'You will lose three months' rent and all the produce from your garden. Are you *sure* you want to leave now?' the man said.

" 'I am sure,' Felix said. 'My father's life is in danger. My wife and my sister may never recover from their horror. We must leave this place immediately.' I never saw any of the De Lacey family again.

"This broke the only link that held me to the world. At first I felt sad, but then I began to feel angry. I did not try to control my feelings of revenge and hatred. One night, I burned the cottage down. Then I began to think about *you*, Frankenstein. It was *your* fault that my life was so unhappy. I decided to punish you.

"Your journal said that you were from Geneva. I had learned from Safie's lessons where Geneva was, so I began to walk to Switzerland. My travels were long and hard. I began in the autumn and traveled through the winter, over frozen mountains. The nearer I got to Geneva, the more deeply did I feel the spirit of revenge in my heart.

"By early spring, I was in Switzerland. One day, I was out in the woods when I heard voices. I hid behind a tree, near a fast mountain stream. A young girl ran out of the trees, laughing, as if running in play. Suddenly her foot slipped, and she fell into the rapid stream. I jumped in after her and pulled her out of the strong current.

"I got her safely to the shore. She was unconscious, and I was trying to revive her when a man approached. He must have been the young girl's father. Grabbing the girl from my arms, he ran toward the woods, and I followed. But when he saw me following, he aimed a gun and fired. He hit me in the shoulder.

"I was in terrible pain. For some weeks, I led a miserable life in the woods. Finally, the wound healed, and I continued walking.

"Two months later, I reached Geneva. It was evening when I arrived. I found a hiding place among the fields and sat down to plot my revenge against you. Just then, a little child burst upon my hiding place.

"As I looked at him, I thought, 'Maybe I can talk to this boy. He hasn't lived long enough to think I'm ugly. Maybe I can educate him as my companion and friend. Then I would not be so lonely.'

"Thinking this, I grabbed the boy's hand. As soon as he saw me, he put his hands in front of his eyes and screamed. 'Child, why are you screaming?' I asked. 'I won't hurt you. Be quiet and listen to me!'

" 'You *monster*!' he cried. 'Let me go, or I'll tell my papa!'

" 'Boy, you will never see your father again. You must come with me.'

" 'Let me go. My papa is Alphonse Frankenstein. He will punish you.'

" '*Frankenstein?* Then you belong to my enemy. You shall be my first victim.' The child struggled and called me names. I grasped his throat to silence him. In a moment he lay dead at my feet.

"When I gazed on my victim, I was filled with excitement. This child belonged to your family. I would show you! I would bring as much misery to you as you had to me!

"As I looked down on the child, I saw something on his clothing. It was a pin with a portrait of a beautiful woman on it. That made me angry again. Such a woman would never be kind to me.

"I walked on. Soon I came to a barn. A pretty young woman was sleeping inside. I bent over her and whispered sweet words of love to her. She moved in her sleep. I knew that if she woke up, she would see me and scream.

"Thanks to the lessons of Felix, I knew something about the law. If the portrait pin were found on her, the police would blame *her* for the boy's death. I slipped it into her pocket. Then I ran away.

"I knew that one day we would meet, Frankenstein. We may not part until you have made a promise to me. I am alone and miserable. No one will associate with me. Only someone who looks like me would be my companion. Frankenstein, you must make a wife for me!"

# Frankenstein Breaks His Promise

When the creature finished speaking, I didn't know what to say. At first I told him that I would not make a wife for him. I was not going to make another monster whose wickedness might harm others.

"Please listen to reason," the creature answered. "I am evil only because I'm so unhappy. If I have company, I won't be so sad. We will not stay near people. They would hate us and want to hurt us. I will take my wife to the vast wilds of South America, far away from anyone."

After he made this promise, I agreed to make a wife for him. I felt that I owed him whatever small happiness I could supply. He said, "Begin your work soon. When you are ready, I shall be there."

I returned home, but I spoke to no one

about my meeting with the creature. How could I? I knew now that I had to keep my promise. If I didn't, the creature would destroy everyone who was close to me.

I found that I couldn't make a female creature without many months of study. Then I read about some new discoveries in England. They could take months off my work. I had to speak to the scientists there. I told my father that I had to go to England for a while. Of course, I didn't say why.

To my surprise, my father thought the trip was a good idea. He had been worried about my sad moods. He felt that travel would do me good and thought that Clerval should meet me on the way. I knew that I couldn't let Henry know what I was planning to do. But how could I say that I didn't want my best friend to travel with me?

Once in England, I went to Oxford University. I spoke with the best scientists and took notes. This information would save me months, maybe years, of work.

Henry and I decided to take a long vacation. We traveled all over for months.

We saw many wonderful places, but thoughts of the monster never left me. I knew that soon I would have to begin making a woman for the monster. The idea made me feel sick.

I also had the feeling that we were being followed. It had been six months since I made my promise to the monster. Would he punish me for this delay? Would he murder my friend? I tried to shake off the thought.

Finally, I found a place to work. It was an island near Scotland. Only five people lived there. On the whole island there were but three miserable huts, and one was vacant. I rented it and got it ready for my work. Henry did not come to the island with me. He decided to visit Ireland. We agreed to meet in a few months.

When I made the first creature, I had high hopes to keep me going. These hopes blinded me to the horror of my work. It was different now. Instead of hope, I had fears. What if she turned out to be even more evil than the first creature? The monster had promised to take his wife away from people. Maybe she would not agree to go! And there was no way to know how she would feel about *him*. She might hate him as everyone else did. Then there would be *two* angry monsters loose in the world!

But what if the creatures did go away together? What if they had children? What terrible things would their children be? I would have created an entire race of monsters! Had I the right to do this?

I groaned and my heart failed within me. On looking up, I saw the monster by the light of the moon at the window. Yes, he had followed me in my travels! He had now come to claim his wife.

Suddenly, I knew that I couldn't go through with my plans. Trembling with passion, I tore to pieces the thing on the table. The wretch saw what I was doing. With a howl of despair, he ran off.

I left the lab and went to my room. I sat there for hours. Suddenly I heard the paddling of oars near the shore. Someone landed near my house. A few minutes later, my door opened and the wretch appeared.

"Go away!" I cried. "I won't do it. I *can't*

make myself do what you want!"

"You dare break your promise to me?" the monster asked. "Shall every man have a wife, and every animal have his mate, and I be alone? I will have my revenge. You will be sorry for what you have done."

"Leave me. I will not change my mind."

"Very well, Frankenstein. I will go. But remember—I shall be with you on your wedding night."

Then he was gone. I saw him get in his boat, which shot across the waters swiftly. All was again silent, but his words still rang in my ears. The night passed, and the sun rose. I spent the morning walking on the beach. Then, exhausted, I fell asleep on the grass and slept the rest of the day.

That night, I returned to my lab and gathered up all the dead body parts and put them into a sack. I took my small boat out to sea. I rowed for hours. Then I threw the terrible things into the water. Feeling tired, I sat back to rest for a few minutes. Then I must have fallen asleep.

When I awoke, it was daylight. I couldn't

see land. The wind was strong, and the waves were high. I had no way of knowing where I was. Somehow I kept the boat from going under. It was hours before the wind died away, and I finally saw land.

I made it to shore. As soon as I landed, several people crowded toward me. "Come with me, right away," one of them said. "I am taking you to a judge, and then to jail."

"*Why?*" I asked in amazement. "Is it the custom of Englishmen to be so rude to strangers?"

"I don't know what the custom of the English may be," said the man. "But it is the custom of the Irish to hate murderers."

My mind was spinning. What could this be about? "I have done no wrong," I said. "I was lost all night in a storm off Scotland."

"Tell that to the judge," the man said.

§10 Frankenstein Loses His Friend

I was soon taken to the judge, an old man with calm and mild manners. About half a dozen men came forward, and the judge selected one. The man told the judge that he had had been out fishing the night before with his son and brother-in-law. When the storm came up, they found they couldn't make it back to the harbor. They tied up at a creek about two miles away.

As the fisherman was walking along the sands, he said he tripped against something and fell. His companions came up to help him. By the light of their lanterns, they found that he had fallen on the body of a man. It was a handsome man, about 25 years old. At first, they thought he had drowned—but his clothes weren't wet. They took him to a nearby cottage. In the light, they saw

that he had been murdered. The marks of the murderer's fingers were still on his neck.

The first part of this story didn't interest me. But when the mark of the fingers was mentioned, I thought of my poor brother.

Other witnesses told of seeing a boat with one man in it push off from the beach. They thought the boat looked very much like the one I had. Several other men talked about my landing. They agreed that the strong wind of last night had probably stopped me from getting away. They thought that I had brought the body from another place.

The judge listened to all of this without saying a word. Then he ordered me to go to the room where the body lay. He wanted to see how I would react to the sight of it.

Entering the room where the body lay, I was led up to the coffin. How can I describe my feelings on seeing it? I still feel the horror. I cannot think about that terrible moment without agony. The lifeless form of Henry Clerval was stretched out before me. I gasped for breath. Throwing myself on the body, I exclaimed, "Has my terrible work cost you also, my dearest Henry, your life? Two I have already destroyed. But you, Clerval, my friend—"

The room around me went black as I passed out and fell to the floor.

A terrible fever followed. For two months I lay at the point of death. I learned later that I called myself the murderer of William, of Justine, and of Clerval. Luckily, I spoke in Italian. Only the judge understood me. But my bitter cries and wails were enough to frighten the other witnesses.

When I began to get better, I saw that I was in a jail cell. After a while, I began to come back to the real world again. Imagine my joy when one day my father came to visit me. I stretched out my hand to him and cried, "Father! Are you safe, then—and Elizabeth—and Ernest?"

My father told me they were well, which raised my spirits. My trial was some weeks later. It was proved that I had been on my Scottish island when my friend's body was found. Thankfully, I was set free.

We had to go through Paris to get to Geneva. While there, I found that I was still too sick to go on. My father and I stayed in Paris so I could rest. Then, a few days before we left Paris for Switzerland, I got a letter from Elizabeth.

She said that she knew our marriage had always been the great dream of my parents. But perhaps I didn't feel the same way. She said that she still loved me. But she was afraid that perhaps I thought of her as a sister. Perhaps, in all my travels, I had met another. She said that if I no longer wanted to get married, she would understand.

How could I tell her of my feelings? The only reason we were not married was that the monster had said, "I shall be with you on your wedding night." Such was my sentence, and on that night I knew he would try to kill me. He would do what he could to tear me from any happiness. Well, so be it. A deadly struggle would take place. If he won, I would be at peace and his power over me would be at an end. If he lost, I would be a free man.

But what *kind* of freedom would I have? It was my fault that William, Justine, and Henry were dead. It was only in my Elizabeth that I possessed a treasure. My sweet and beloved Elizabeth! I read and reread her letter. I thought about whether my marriage would hasten my death. Then I realized that the creature might kill me even if I *didn't* get married. I decided, then, that we would get married as soon as possible.

I wrote to Elizabeth. My letter was calm and loving. I told her that I had one secret, a terrible one. "When revealed to you, it will chill you with horror. I will tell you this tale the day after our marriage. My sweet Elizabeth, there must be perfect confidence between us. But until then, please do not mention this secret," I wrote.

My father and I returned to Geneva. We began to get ready for the wedding. All the time we were making our plans, I kept thinking of what the monster had said. I bought some guns and knives. The monster might be dead. But if he were alive, I would be ready for him. I was not going to die without a fight on my wedding night!

We had a wonderful wedding, followed by a large party at my father's. We took a boat ride to the city of Evian, where we would begin our honeymoon. Those were the last moments of my life that I was happy.

§11 Another Loss for Frankenstein

It was 8:00 P.M. when we landed. For a short time, we walked on the shore, enjoying the fading light. Then we went to our room at the inn. We looked out at the lovely scene of waters, woods, and mountains.

The wind, which had fallen in the south, now rose up in the west. The moon was beginning to descend. The clouds swept across it and dimmed its rays. The lake reflected the beauty of the busy skies. Then suddenly, heavy rain began to fall.

I had been calm during the day. But as night fell, a thousand fears rose in my mind. I was anxious and watchful. My right hand grasped a pistol that was hidden in my pocket. Every sound terrified me. But I resolved I would not back off of the fight until my own life or that of the monster was ended.

I passed an hour in this state of mind. Then suddenly I thought how fearful the fight I expected would be to my wife. I decided to check each room in the hotel. I would face the monster anywhere else but in our room. I left as Elizabeth was getting ready for bed.

I was walking up and down the halls of the inn when I heard a shrill and dreadful scream. As I listened, the terrible truth rushed into my mind. The monster wasn't planning to kill *me*—it was *Elizabeth* he was after! The scream was repeated, and I rushed to the room.

Great God! Why did I not then die! Why am I here to tell this terrible story? Elizabeth was there, dead, thrown across the bed. Her head was hanging down, and her pale face was half covered by her hair. No matter which way I turned, all I could see was Elizabeth, flung by the murderer on her bridal bed. Could I see this and live? Alas! Life is strong and clings even when it is most hated. I fell to the ground in a faint.

When I came to, I was surrounded by the

people of the inn. Their faces showed terror, but their horrified feelings were but a dim shadow of my own.

I rushed toward Elizabeth and took her in my arms. But what I now held was no longer the Elizabeth whom I had loved. The mark of the fiend's hand was on her neck, and she was no longer breathing.

Just then, I happened to look up. The pale yellow light of the moon lit the room. I saw at the open window the hideous and hated monster. A grin was on his face as he pointed toward the corpse of my wife. I rushed toward the window, drawing a pistol from my pocket. I fired, but he escaped. Running as fast as lightning, he plunged into the lake.

Men from the hotel helped me look for the monster. We used boats and nets, but we couldn't find him. After several hours, we returned to the inn. Most of my companions believed that I had only imagined the fleeing monster. Yet some of them set off among the woods to continue the search. Of course, they found nothing.

I felt a sadness I had never known before.

The death of William, the execution of Justine, the murder of Clerval, and now the killing of my wife—it was all so horrible. I began to worry about my last remaining loved ones. Even now my father might be writhing under the creature's grasp! Ernest might be dead at his feet! I decided to return to Geneva right away.

My father and Ernest were still alive. But when I told my father what had happened, it was too much for him. I think he had loved Elizabeth more than any of the Frankenstein family. His heart was broken. A few days later, he died in my arms.

What, after that, became of me? I do not know. They called me mad. For many months, I heard, I was kept in a madhouse.

When I came back to my right mind, I thought about revenge. I began to think about the best way to get it. I decided to go to a judge in the town. I told him that I knew who the destroyer of my family was. I said that I wanted all necessary means used to find the murderer.

I told the judge the whole story. He

listened to me with attention and kindness. I knew that I was taking a chance. Anyone hearing the tale would be sure I was out of my mind. Yet, I had to tell the truth. I showed the judge that I *couldn't* be mad— all the parts of the story fit together too well for that. Thank God, he believed me.

"But what can you do about it?" asked the judge. "I would help you if I could. But it has been some months since the creature's crimes. He could be anywhere. He followed you across Europe. The weather does not seem to bother him. And he is stronger than any man."

"It doesn't matter," I told the judge. "I will go after him alone. He is never far from me. He stays near me to enjoy all the sadness he has brought to my life. He laughs at what he has done. I will find the evil creature, and I will kill him. Or I will spend the rest of my life trying!"

§12 The Chase

My first decision was to leave Geneva forever. When I was happy and loved, my country was dear to me. Now, in my sorrow, it became hateful. I got together a sum of money, together with a few jewels that had been my mother's, and left.

As night approached, I found myself at the cemetery where William, Elizabeth, and my father rested. Entering it, I went to their graves. Everything was silent except the leaves in the trees. The night became very dark. The spirits of the dead seemed to cast a shadow around my head.

I knelt on the grass and kissed the earth. "By all that is holy," I exclaimed, "I swear to find the demon who caused this misery! Then I shall fight him to the death. To this I pledge my life. I call on you, spirits of the dead, to help me in my work. Let the monster drink deep of agony. Let him feel that despair that now torments me!"

In the stillness of the night I was answered by a loud and fiendish laugh. The mountains echoed the laugh until it died away. Then a hated voice, close to my ear, spoke in a loud whisper. "I am happy now, Frankenstein. You have decided to live, and you will be unhappy for the rest of your life. You will be alone—just as I am." Then it laughed again.

Just then, the moon broke through the clouds. I could see the monster, running so fast that no man could catch him. I tried to follow him, but he left me far behind.

Since that night, I have chased the monster all over the world. He stays away from towns and cities. But sometimes the peasants, frightened after seeing him, tell me which way he went. Sometimes he leaves some mark to guide me. I suppose he fears that if I lose track of him, I will give up and die. He wants me to continue to live— and suffer.

Once I saw him get on a ship going to the Black Sea. I took my passage on the same ship, but he escaped. I know not how.

My life was indeed hateful to me. It was only during sleep that I could taste joy. In my dreams, I saw my friends, my wife, and my beloved country. Again I saw the good face of my father and heard the silver tones of my Elizabeth's voice. And in dreams I saw Clerval enjoying health and youth.

I do not know what the monster felt. Sometimes he wrote messages on the bark of trees or cut them in stone. "My power over you is still strong," said one. Another time, he wrote, "Follow me. I go to the ice of the north. There you will feel the misery of cold and frost, which do not bother me. You will find a dead rabbit near here. Eat it and be refreshed. Come closer, my enemy! We have yet to fight for our lives. But you must suffer through many hard and miserable hours before then."

As I got farther north, I found one last note from the monster. It said: "Get ready! The worst is still ahead of you. Gather furs and plenty of food. We are going to a cold, icy place. I will laugh as you suffer."

I bought a sled and some dogs to pull it. Soon I came to a small village on the seashore. When I asked the villagers about the creature, they said they had seen him. A giant had arrived just the night before. He stole guns, the villagers' winter food supply, a sled, and some trained dogs. Then he headed north, much to the joy of the villagers. He had gone in a direction that led to no land. They thought that he would soon be killed by the breaking of the ice or frozen by the eternal snow.

After a short rest, I got ready for my journey. I traded my land sled for one made for the frozen ocean. I bought food for myself and the dogs. Then I went after him.

I spent three weeks chasing him. Once, after one of the dogs died, I almost gave up. Then suddenly I saw a dark spot on the white plain. I could just make out the shape of a sled. Oh, what hope came back to my heart!

I fed the dogs and let them rest for an hour. Then I went on. I could still see the sled ahead of me. After two days, I could see my enemy no more than a mile away. My heart beat fast within me.

Just then, the wind rose and the sea roared. Like a strong earthquake, the ice split and cracked with a loud sound. In a few minutes, cold blue water separated me from my enemy. I was left drifting on a piece of ice that was getting smaller. I began preparing for a hideous death.

I floated on this piece of ice for many hours. All but one of my dogs died. I was close to death myself. Then I saw your ship. I had no idea that ships ever came so far north. To make oars, I quickly destroyed part of my sled. With great effort, I was able to move my icy raft toward your ship.

You probably wondered why I asked you where your ship was going. As I have said, I will never give up my search for the creature. If you had been going south, I would not have gone with you. Instead, I would have asked you to give me a small boat. But you are headed north—where I am sure the creature has gone. That is why I am happy to have come on board.

And that is my story. I have lost the monster. I would ask you to help me find him, but that wouldn't be fair. You want to go on to the North Pole. It is the dream of your life. I ask only this: If I die, and you find the monster, *show him no mercy*. He may talk sweetly. He may tell you that everyone has treated him badly. But he is the king of liars.

His words may begin to change your mind. But remember William, Justine, Henry, Elizabeth, and my father. All of them died because of him. Don't stop to think. *Kill him!* Only then will my soul rest in peace.

Closing Letters

To: Mrs. Saville, England
August 26, 17__

Dear Sister,
    You have read this strange story, Margaret. Does it make your blood run cold, as it does mine? The question is: Do I believe the story? Frankenstein showed me letters written by Felix and Safie, the young people in the cottage. And we saw the monster from our ship. I cannot doubt his story.
    Frankenstein saw that I was taking notes while he talked. When I showed them to him, he made some changes. He wanted to make sure I told the story correctly. Then I asked how he gave life to the monster. He said, "Are you mad? Didn't you learn from my tale? Never again will such a creature be made! I will take the secret to my grave. There is only one more thing I must do in my life," Frankenstein went on. "I must find and kill the monster. Then I can die in peace."

September 2

My Dear Sister,

I fear we are lost. The ice has closed around us again. Everywhere we look we see mountains of white ice. The men want a promise from me. If we can get out of this ice, they want me to sail back for home. I must give up my dream, for I do not wish to risk the lives of others.

Meanwhile, Frankenstein's health is failing. He grows weaker each day. He seems alive only when he talks of his hunt for the monster. Then, his eyes shine, and he tries to get out of bed. But he is too weak.

The ice is all around us. I don't know if you will ever get this letter.

I send my love.

September 12

The ice has broken! I went down to Frankenstein's cabin to tell him the news. He sat up in his bed. "Then you are turning back?" he asked.

"Yes, I must. I have promised the men."

Frankenstein shook my hand. "I wish you

well, Walton," he said. "God keep you safe on your trip home. But I cannot go with you. I am still weak, but heaven will give me strength. The creature must die."

With this, Frankenstein tried to get out of bed. When he fell back and passed out, I thought he had died. But in a few minutes, his eyes opened again.

"I'm afraid I'm dying," he said. "And it hurts to know that the monster still lives. I have thought about my life. I think I did no wrong. My reason for creating the monster was good: I wanted to help humankind.

"And I think I was right when I would not make a wife for him. He had shown what he was like. He had killed William and had caused Justine's death. I couldn't be sure that he wouldn't kill again. And with a whole race of these creatures, who would be safe?

"I wish I could ask you to take up my hunt for the monster, but I can't. You have your own life to live. But if you should ever come across the evil creature, kill it! Don't stop for a second. And now . . ."

His voice faded away. He lay back on the bed. He tried to speak again but could not. Then his eyes closed forever, and a gentle smile passed away from his lips.

I must stop writing now. Something is going on below decks. I hear a sound like a human voice, but somehow different. I must go see what is happening.

Great God, what I have just seen! I am still dizzy just thinking about it.

I went to the cabin where the body of Frankenstein lay. Over him hung a form that I cannot find words to describe. His long hair was black, shiny, and ragged, and it hid his face. One hand was reaching out, as if to touch Frankenstein. I saw the hand. It was yellow and wrinkled, like a mummy's.

He heard me come in and ran toward the window. Never in my life have I seen such a creature. I cannot find the words to tell how ugly and horrible it was. I had to turn away.

Remembering what Frankenstein had asked me to do, I called on him to stay. He looked at me in surprise. Then he looked back at the dead body of his creator.

"With this victim, it is ended. Oh, Frankenstein, I am sorry for all the misery I caused you. Alas! You are cold. You cannot answer me." The creature gave a cry of sadness.

I looked at the monster. I almost felt sorry for him. Then I remembered all the lives this creature had taken. I was afraid, yet I had to speak.

"Being sorry won't help," I said. "It's too late. If you'd had any good in you, Frankenstein would still be alive."

"Do you think I wanted to be evil?" the monster asked. "Do you think the cries of poor Clerval were music to my ears? I am a gentle creature. My heart was made to receive love—not to be filled with hate! When Frankenstein destroyed my wife, I went mad with sadness. I wanted to give Frankenstein a taste of the unhappiness he had given me.

"After the murder of Clerval, I went back to Switzerland. My heart was broken. I felt pity for Frankenstein, and I hated myself.

"Then I heard of Frankenstein's plan to marry. How dare he be happy, when I was so alone? The madness came over me again. I couldn't stop myself. Do you know the pain it caused me to kill Elizabeth? I can still hear her cries. But I was like Satan cast out of heaven. Evil had become my God. And now it is ended. There is my last victim!"

I was at first touched by his words. But then I remembered that Frankenstein had said he was the king of liars. "Wretch!" I said. "The only thing you are sorry for is that you can no longer torment him!"

"I know why you think that. But you have heard only Frankenstein's side of the story. I always hoped that someone would see beyond my outside looks. I wanted someone to love me, but no one did. Why do you not hate Felix, who drove me from his door? Why do you not hate the father who shot the rescuer of his child? No, they are good beings. I was made to be spurned, kicked, and trampled on. Even now, I cry for Frankenstein. You see, I am not just a creature of evil. I am what Frankenstein and the world have made me.

"Don't worry," he went on. "I am finished with evil. It is over now. No one else will die at my hands. It is now time for me to die. And I will take care of that quickly.

"I shall leave your ship on the ice raft that brought me here. I will float away to the land of ice and snow. Without food, even I shall die. I shall die as I lived: alone, without love, and hated by all."

The creature looked down at the body of Frankenstein. "Goodbye, my creator," it said. "I made a hell of your life. But it was nothing like the hell I had to live through."

Saying this, the monster jumped through the open window of the cabin. He landed on the ice raft that lay close to the ship. He was soon carried away by the waves and lost in darkness and distance.